DIGBY O'DAY

and the Great Diamond Robbery

Text copyright © 2014 by Shirley Hughes
Illustrations copyright © 2014 by Clara Vulliamy

First U.S. edition 2015

Library of Congress Catalog Card Number 2014951400
ISBN 978-0-7636-7445-8

LEO 20 19 18 17 16 15
10 9 8 7 6 5 4 3 2 1

Printed in Heshan, Guangdong, China

This book was typeset in Bodoni Antiqua.
The illustrations were done in pencil, ink, and digital collage.

Candlewick Press
99 Dover Street
Somerville, Massachusetts 02144

visit us at www.candlewick.com

DiGBY O'DAY

and the Great Diamond Robbery

Shirley Hughes

illustrated by

Clara Vulliamy

CANDLEWICK PRESS

Contents

And some fun extras at the back!

MEET DIGBY AND PERCY!

Digby O'Day is always ready for adventure, as is his good friend Percy. And where better to find adventure than on vacation! We talked with Digby and Percy about their vacation triumphs and disasters:

Hello, Digby and Percy— thank you for talking with us. First, tell us about your perfect vacation.

DIGBY: *That would be staying at the Hotel Splendide in Brightsea, strolling along the beach and getting plenty of fresh sea air.*

PERCY: *Oh, yes, with ballroom dancing in the evenings.*

And who would be your perfect vacation companion?

DIGBY: *Percy and I have had our ups and downs, but I can't imagine a vacation without him.*

PERCY: *I second that!*

What about the worst vacation you've ever had?

DIGBY: *When we were young, we went on a school trip and Percy lost his suitcase. I had to lend him my spare pajamas!*

PERCY: *It was pretty awful when you were sick on the bus, too.*

What do you always pack in your suitcase?

DIGBY: *My hot-water bottle, a choice of dress ties, and my copy of* 100 Country Walks.

PERCY: *Plenty of treats.*

Which do you prefer, the seaside or the mountains?

DIGBY: *The seaside. I don't want to risk engine trouble on the steep mountain roads.*

PERCY: *Me too. Cotton candy on the pier and a trip in a paddleboat!*

And finally, is there anything worse than getting sand in your sandwiches?

DIGBY: *Having your tent blown away in the night.*

PERCY: *Arriving too late for supper and finding the hotel dining room closed.*

We agree—that sounds awful. Thank you, Digby and Percy!

Mr. Canteloe

Likes:
walking by the sea
stargazing
playing chess

Peaches Meow

Likes:
jewelry
singing
limousines

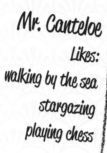

Detective Inspector Sharply
Chief inspector for Brightsea Police

Stripy Sid & Alley the Claws
Shady characters

Peaches Meow's entourage:
her manager
her secretary
her press agent
her hairdresser
and her personal trainer

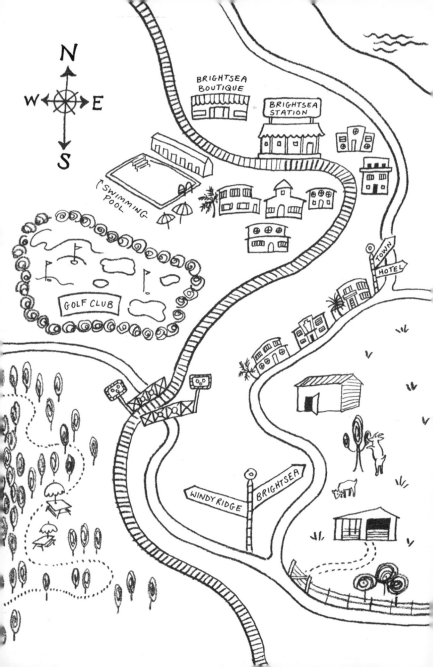

Chapter One

One fine summer morning, Digby O'Day said to his friend Percy, "I've decided that it's time to take a little trip. Would you accompany me, Percy?"

"You bet," said Percy. "Shall we take the tent and go camping?"

"No, I'm thinking of something a bit more luxurious. I'm booking us in at the Hotel Splendide in Brightsea!"

"The Hotel Splendide! That's one of the very poshest hotels on the coast! Won't it be terribly expensive?"

"Never mind that," Digby replied nonchalantly. "I've been saving up for a long while now, and it's time we had a bit of a treat."

"I'd better pack my bow tie," Percy said.

"Oh, yes," said Digby. "And of course we will have to take our dinner jackets to change into in the evening."

"Oh, dear!" said Percy. "I only have the one that belonged to my uncle Gus! I'm afraid it's a bit moth-eaten and has a couple of gravy stains. . . ."

"Never mind. Give it a bit of a wash, Percy, and you'll look fine. Don't forget, you're one of the best ballroom dancers I know—why, you've even won competitions!"

"I'll do my best not to let you down," said Percy bravely.

They both set to work to give
Digby's car a good clean, polishing
the bodywork until it shone.

7

It wasn't long before they were driving happily toward Brightsea. They had chosen a quiet side road that had more scenic views than the main road and very little traffic.

They were cruising merrily along when suddenly another car zoomed up behind them, seemingly out of nowhere.

It followed closely, almost touching their back bumper, then pulled out and shot past them with inches to spare. There might have been a disastrous crash if Percy hadn't reacted instantly by grabbing the steering wheel.

Digby's car shot up a bank at the side of the road and came to a jolting stop, narrowly missing the fence.

The other car
was already
roaring away
into the
distance.

They sat for a while, stunned with
shock.

"That was a narrow escape!"
muttered Digby at last.

"Demons! Road hogs!" shouted
Percy furiously. "Did you see their
license plate?"

"No, unfortunately. I was too busy trying to get out of their way. All I saw was a driver and one passenger. They both had scarves pulled up, so I couldn't see their faces properly."

17

"No good trying to report them for dangerous driving, then," said Percy. "They should be fined or sent to prison! It's a *DISGRACE*!"

They continued on their journey at a careful pace, feeling very upset.

Chapter Two

They soon cheered up when they saw the Hotel Splendide. It was very grand indeed, high up on a cliff overlooking the sea.

A man in a fancy uniform with
many gold buttons stood at the main
entrance.

When Digby and Percy drove up,
the man glanced down his nose at
Digby's car, which was now covered in
dust and mud, and said, "You'll find
a parking space around the back, sir.
Do you need someone to help with
your luggage?"

"No, thanks. We can manage,"
Digby answered as casually as he could.

Most rooms at the Hotel Splendide were impressively large.

But Digby and Percy's room was small and on the top floor at the back, overlooking the parking lot.

As soon as they had
unpacked and made
themselves look as
dressed up as possible,
they went downstairs.

They found the hotel lobby
full of people. TV reporters, press
photographers, and hotel staff were
bustling about everywhere. "What's
happening?" Percy asked a waiter
scurrying past.

"We're expecting a very important guest, sir," he replied. "The pop star Peaches Meow!"

As they were speaking, a huge white limousine drew up outside and Peaches herself made a dramatic entrance.

She was followed by her manager, secretary, press agent, hairdresser, and personal trainer.

"Peaches Meow!" gasped Percy. "I've been a fan of hers for years. Thank heavens I remembered to pack my best bow tie!"

Digby was unimpressed. And he was very put out when a pushy press photographer told him to get out of the way because he wanted to take a picture.

Peaches posed briefly in a blaze of
camera flashes, then the crowd parted
to allow her to sweep into the elevator
and disappear.

"What a fuss!" said Digby. "Let's get out of here and take a walk, Percy."

Chapter Three

Digby and Percy scrambled down the cliff path, which brought them onto the beach. It was high tide, and a brisk wind was blowing, making the waves choppy.

"Ah, fresh air!" said Digby,
breathing deeply. "This is more like
it! Let's take a walk along the jetty."

There were very few people out
because everyone had gone up to the
Hotel Splendide, hoping to catch a
glimpse of Peaches Meow. As they set
off along the jetty, they could see only
one solitary gentleman walking far
out ahead of them.

Spray from the incoming tide
flew up and drenched them as they
struggled along, heads down against
the wind.

They were a good distance from the shore when Percy anxiously clutched Digby's arm and pointed. The gentleman ahead of them had disappeared!

They ran as fast as they could to
the spot where they had last seen him
and peered into the sea below. They
saw him struggling in the waves. He
had been blown over the side and was
hanging on desperately to the bottom
rung of an iron ladder. His cries for
help were lost in the strong wind.

Digby reacted immediately. He stripped off his jacket and made his way down the ladder.

Once he slipped and nearly lost his footing, but he managed to save himself. Percy followed cautiously, close behind.

Now the gentleman
was thrashing
in the waves.

Every so often
he disappeared
altogether . . .

then came
up again,
gasping for air.

44

Percy grasped the back of Digby's belt and hung on for dear life. Digby, clinging to the ladder with one hand, reached out as far as he dared with the other.

45

Twice he managed to grasp the gentleman by the arm, and twice the gentleman slipped away. Then at last their hands met and Digby pulled with all his might.

Now he had the gentleman by
both arms and, with a huge effort,
managed to yank him up onto the
bottom rung of the ladder, where
they both hung, gulping and spewing
up seawater.

"You have saved my life!" the
gentleman said when (sometime later)
all three of them were safely back
on the jetty, recovering a little and
wringing out their wet clothes.

"I am not a strong swimmer, and without your bravery, I would almost certainly have drowned."

When they parted, he shook them both warmly by the hand and asked for their names and where they were staying.

Chapter Four

Digby and Percy were in the hotel lounge, where afternoon tea was being served, when a letter arrived from the gentleman they had saved from drowning.

He introduced himself as Mr. Gerald Canteloe, thanked them again, and invited them to lunch the following day at his house just across the bay.

"Of course we must accept," said Digby. "It will be interesting to meet him again in more pleasant circumstances."

That evening they were both tired. Digby wanted to go to bed early, but Percy insisted on staying up to see Peaches Meow. She swept into the hotel dining room wearing a silver satin dress and a smile as dazzling as her diamond necklace.

"She looks like a princess!" whispered Percy.

"She certainly knows how to make an entrance," said Digby drily. "Those diamonds must be worth a fortune!"

The next morning, they set out to walk to Mr. Canteloe's house. It was a lovely old place overlooking the sea.

After an excellent lunch, he showed
them the turret where he kept his
telescope for gazing at the stars.

Then he took them downstairs,
through the kitchen to the cellar,
where there was a heavy door,
securely locked and barred.

"This house was once used by smugglers," he told them. "Beyond this door is a secret passage that leads to a cave in the cliffs. That's where those rascals used to stash forbidden goods, smuggled in at night by boat.

At high tide it's completely cut off and very damp, so we can't go down there now. But if you would like to see it, come over again tomorrow evening!"

"This visit has turned out to be a great deal more eventful than we expected," said Digby as they strolled back to the hotel.

"Maybe we'll find some treasure!" said Percy.

Chapter Five

That night Digby could not get to sleep. He lay awake for a long time, thinking over the day's events and listening to Percy's snores. The hotel was very quiet.

But then he thought he heard a faint sound—a scratching noise that seemed to be coming from the roof overhead. He listened. It stopped, then came again.

He got out of bed and tiptoed to the open window. The parking lot below, brightly lit by security lights, was deserted. He leaned out and looked up, but he could see nothing. He waited and cocked his head, listening intently. But now the noise had stopped altogether.

"Seagulls, I suppose," he muttered. Then he drew the curtains tight, scampered back into bed, pulled the covers over his head, and fell into a deep sleep.

Chapter Six

The next morning, Digby and Percy came down late for breakfast and found the hotel in an uproar. Police cars were parked outside, and a crowd of agitated guests was gathered in the lobby. In the middle of it all was Peaches Meow, in hysterics.

"Whatever has happened?" Digby asked the receptionist.

"I'm afraid there was a robbery last night, sir," she replied.

"A great many valuables were taken, including Miss Meow's diamond necklace. Two cat burglars managed to get in through a window without waking the guests.

"Luckily someone spotted them
as they were making their getaway.
The Brightsea Police gave chase, but
unfortunately they lost them."

"Scoundrels!" exclaimed Percy.
"Poor Peaches! What a terrible
experience for her!"

"I thought I heard something on
the roof last night," said Digby, "but
I figured it was seagulls."

That evening they were only too relieved to escape the turmoil at the hotel and walk over to Mr. Canteloe's house again, where he welcomed them, eager to hear all the news about the robbery.

Then he produced two big old-
fashioned keys and led them down
to the cellar. A dank, musty smell
greeted them as he unlocked the
door to the secret passage, which
swung open.

75

Shining his flashlight, Mr. Canteloe
went ahead down a narrow flight of
stairs, which were slimy and damp.
Digby followed behind him. Percy
came last, tightly clutching the back
of Digby's jacket.

The stairs soon gave way to a passage roughly cut out of the rock, sloping steeply downward. In some places the ceiling was so low they had to make their way bent over.

By now they could feel the tang of cold sea air. Then the slope flattened out and they found they were walking on sand and pebbles. They could hear the wash of the tide outside.

They had just reached the cave when Mr. Canteloe's flashlight suddenly cut out, and they were plunged into darkness, broken only by a faint glimmer of moonlight ahead.

"Sorry—the battery's failed," said Mr. Canteloe.

"I don't like it here," whispered Percy, holding on to Digby more tightly.

"It's all right—just follow me!"

They inched forward, and the
passage opened up into a cavernous
space around them. As they moved
into the cave, they heard a scuffling
sound and stealthy footsteps. They
were not alone!

For a moment, they stood stock
still. As their eyes adjusted to the dim
light, they looked around and saw two
figures crouching over something half
buried in the sand.

Digby stepped forward.

"Who are you? What do you want?" he called out, his voice brave and steady.

There was a pause. The figures straightened up and looked toward them. The friends could see two pairs of eyes, glittering in the dark.

Then the figures sprang at Digby,
making for the entrance to the cave.
Digby grappled with one of them for
a moment, but the intruder wrenched
free. Digby tried to clutch at the
fleeing figure's sleeve, but there was
a ripping sound as he lost his footing
and fell heavily backward
into a puddle.

As Digby's two friends ran to his
aid, the intruders seized their chance
to escape. With a rush of scurrying
movement, they were off, splashing
through the shallow water at the
mouth of the cave and on up the
deserted beach.

The three friends chased after
them, slipping on loose pebbles,
vaulting over breakwaters, stumbling
in the dark. Poor Mr. Canteloe ran
bravely, but he was gasping for
breath, and Percy's legs were too
short for him to keep up.

The fugitives were too fast for them. They ran effortlessly and seemed to be able to see in the dark. In no time, they had disappeared into the sand dunes and were gone.

As the three friends went back into the cave, Mr. Canteloe nearly tripped over something. Looking down, he saw packages wrapped in plastic bags strewn about the cave floor.

"Whatever . . . ?" he began.

But Digby had spotted something else. It was the sleeve that he had ripped from the intruder's shirt during their struggle, now lying in a puddle. He picked it up and put it into his pocket, and then . . .

there was a loud cry from Percy!

He had found something too,
lying half hidden in the pebbles—
something that sparkled even in the
dim light. He grabbed it and held it
up in triumph.

A diamond necklace!

Chapter Seven

It was Peaches Meow's necklace, all right! And when they swiftly set to work opening the packages, they found that they were full of all sorts of other valuables.

Mr. Canteloe said, "These were almost certainly stolen from the hotel last night. Those crooks must have hidden their loot in the cave and were coming back to collect it when the coast was clear."

"Thank heavens you spotted Miss Meow's necklace, Percy!" said Digby. "It might have been lost forever, washed away by the tide. We must return it at once and notify the police!"

They caused a great sensation when they arrived back at the hotel, just as the sun was rising, carrying the stolen valuables. A huge cheer went up from the guests. Detective Inspector Sharply, who was in charge of the case, congratulated them and shook them warmly by the hand.

At that moment, a police car tore up to the main entrance of the hotel, sirens blazing.

Two police officers got out and marched a pair of handcuffed suspects into the foyer. They were both struggling and hissing horribly.

"We arrested them for dangerous driving while trying to leave Brightsea," explained one of the police officers, "and we think there may be other charges."

Inspector Sharply turned to Digby and Percy.

"Do you recognize these suspects?" he asked.

"Yes! They are the two rogues we discovered in the cave with all these valuables," Digby told them. "I can prove it!"

And he pulled the sleeve from his pocket.

"I ripped this off before they both ran away!"

It was an exact match.

WANTED

ALLEY THE CLAWS

REWARD

WANTED

STRIPY SID

REWARD

"These two criminals are well known to us as Alley the Claws and Stripy Sid," said Inspector Sharply. "They are suspected of committing robberies all along the coast. Now we have evidence to bring them to trial."

Just then Peaches Meow rushed
down the stairs.

"My necklace is safe at last!" she
cried. "I thought I would never see
it again! Oh, thank you, thank you!"
And she threw her arms around
Percy and kissed him. Percy was quite
overcome.

When things had calmed down
a little, Digby took Mr. Canteloe's
arm and led him outside to a quiet
spot overlooking the sea. They sat
in silence for a while, looking at the
incoming tide.

"It's good to have a little peace and quiet at last," said Digby. "That's what we came here for, after all."

"I hope you'll come and visit us again when things are back to normal," Mr. Canteloe replied.

"You are most kind," said Digby, "although I think next time we take a break, we might try somewhere inland."

The manager of the hotel and all his staff were in the lobby to see Digby and Percy off when they departed the following morning.

"It's been an honor to have you here, sirs," he said. "It was entirely through your courage that Miss Meow's necklace and all the other valuables were found and returned. The reputation of the hotel has been saved. Please come back and visit us again soon—free of charge, of course!"

The doorman snapped his fingers to summon one of the staff to bring Digby's car around to the front entrance, then put their luggage in the trunk.

"We've had it cleaned and polished for you, sir," he said. "And may I say what a great pleasure it is to see a car like yours on the road these days."

"Well, it turned out all right in the
end," said Digby as they set off on the
coast road toward home.

But Percy wasn't listening. He was
in a dream, clutching a large framed
photograph of Peaches Meow to his
chest.

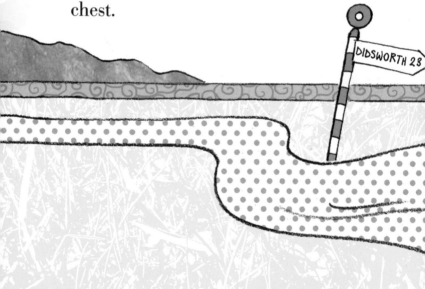

DIDSWORTH 23

It was signed: "To Percy—my hero!
With love and kisses from Peaches
Meow."

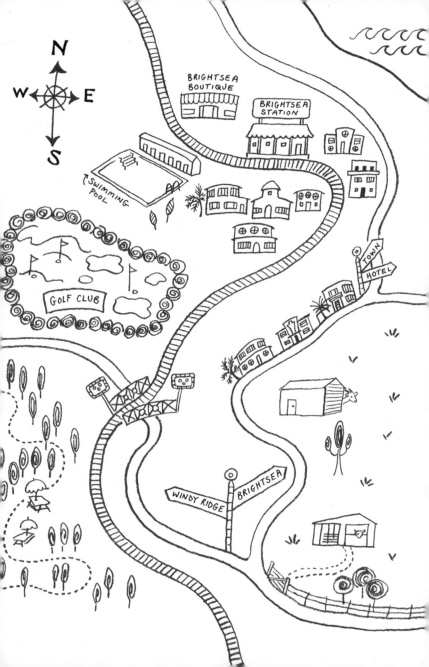

DIGBY'S WORLD

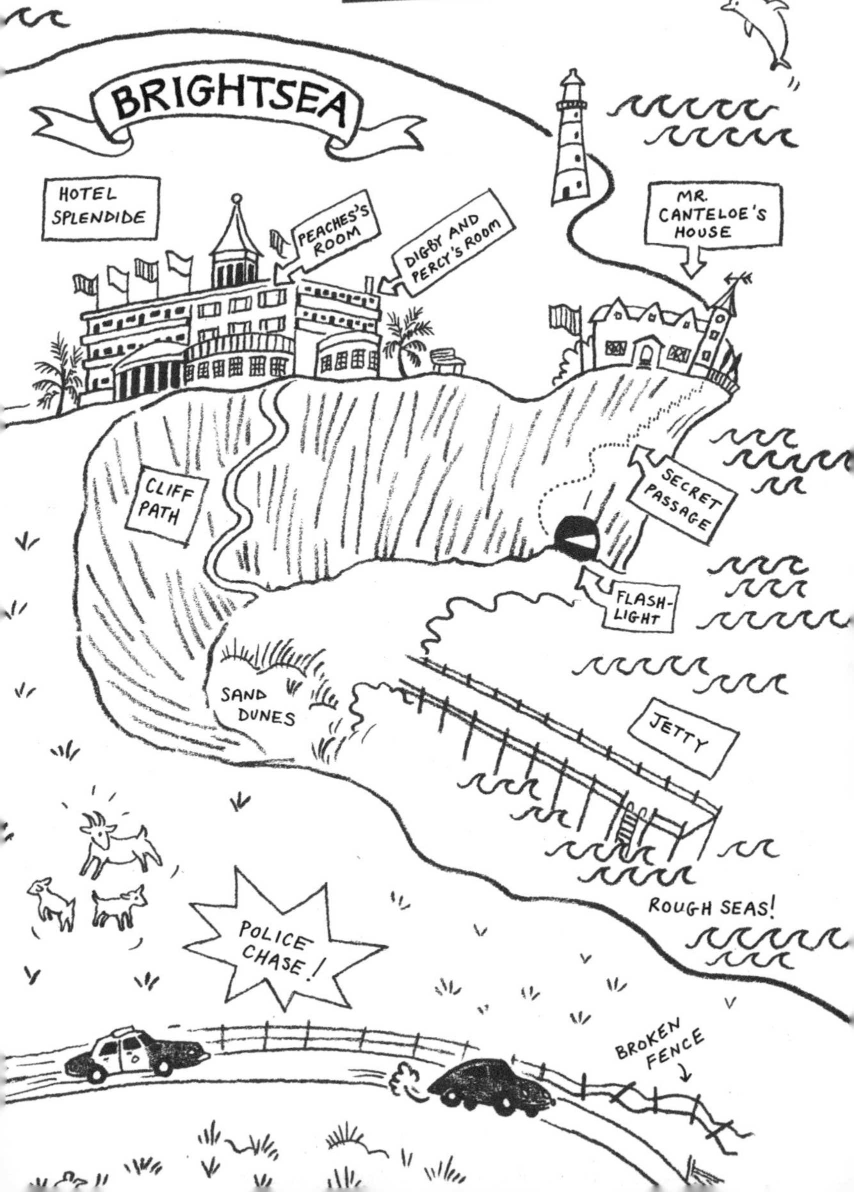

AND NOW MEET
Shirley Hughes and
Clara Vulliamy.

Shirley is Clara's mum, and together they have created Digby and Percy's adventures. We thought we'd ask them about their favorite vacations:

Hello, Shirley and Clara!

Can you tell us about your perfect vacation?

SHIRLEY: *Mine would be with friends and family in a peaceful spot, quite near to home.*

CLARA: *And mine would be a winter vacation with plenty of snow.*

And who would be your perfect vacation companion?

SHIRLEY: *Clara.*   CLARA: *Mum!*

What's the worst vacation you've ever had?

SHIRLEY: *In a primitive cottage with an outdoor toilet and lots of spiders.*

CLARA: *When I capsized in a canoe without having packed a dry change of clothes.*

What do you always pack in your suitcase?

SHIRLEY: *My sketchbook.*

CLARA: *My* Classic Cars *magazines.*

What do you like to do on your vacation?

SHIRLEY: *Sunbathe, visit art galleries, lurk about with my sketchbook.*

CLARA: *Eat an ice-cream sundae, play miniature golf, and speed along on a zip line (but not all at the same time).*

And finally, is there anything worse than getting sand in your sandwiches?

SHIRLEY: *Being marooned at an airport with my flight indefinitely delayed.*

CLARA: *Finding myself in a field with an angry bull.*

YIKES! Thank you so much, Shirley and Clara.

Mysterious Maze

Digby, Percy, and Mr. Canteloe
need to collect the missing loot before
Stripy Sid and Alley the Claws get their paws on it!

Help them find their way through the maze with your finger
and get to the stolen valuables in time!

Now draw a WANTED poster of
your own dastardly villains!
What are their names, and
what do they look like?

ALLEY THE CLAWS
REWARD

STRIPY SID
REWARD

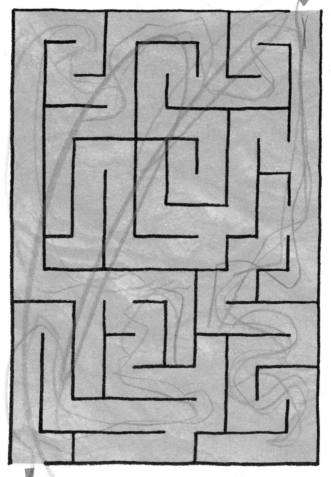

The Digby O'Day Quiz

Digby has written a quiz to test you!
How much can you remember
about Digby O'Day and the Great Diamond Robbery?

1. Who did Percy's dinner jacket once belong to?

2. What's on the license plate of the black car that forces Digby off the road?

3. What color is Peaches Meow's limousine?

4. True or false: Peaches Meow travels with her hairdresser.

5. True or false: Mr. Canteloe rescues Digby from the sea.

6. What is Mr. Canteloe's first name?

7. What book is Percy reading at the Hotel Splendide?

8. How many burglars are there?

9. What does Digby rip off one of the burglars?

10. True or false: Digby finds Peaches's necklace in the cave.

11. What does Peaches Meow give to Percy?

12. On the map of Brightsea, what is next door to the train station?

If you enjoyed

DIGBY O'DAY
and the
Great Diamond Robbery,

then you'll love Digby and Percy's
next adventure,

DIGBY O'DAY
Up, Up, and Away!

Turn the page for the first chapter. . . .

DiGBY O'DAY

Up, Up, and Away!

Digby O'Day was very proud of his car. He cleaned and polished it every weekend, and his friend Percy came to help.

One Saturday, when they were giving it an extra shine, Digby said, "This is a really good car, but one day I'd like to try a different form of transportation."

"It still runs well," said Percy encouragingly. But he added, "As long as you don't try to pass in the fast lane."

Digby's car had given them trouble recently when, during a slow crawl home from shopping, the engine had failed during a traffic jam and he and Percy had ended up pushing it all the way home.

Don Barrakan at the garage had repaired it in no time, of course. But even so, there were times when Digby daydreamed about being effortlessly airborne—up, up, and away!

DiGBY O'DAY

Digby's irritating next-door neighbor, Lou Ella, bought an expensive new car every year. She liked new things: new clothes, new cars, new furniture, and new kitchen cabinets.

She even changed her pets quite often. She had already tired of her goldfish because she thought he was boring and her Siamese cat because he sharpened his claws on the carpet and her hamster because he kept her awake at night running and running on his little wheel. She had given them all away, one by one.

Now she had bought a parrot, and she claimed she was teaching him to speak. His name was Ariel.

She had spent a lot of money on a beautiful parrot perch with ladders, bells, and swings, which she had placed in the bay window of her house, so that passersby could see her interesting new pet.

And she devoted a lot of time to grooming him, glossing up his feathers and manicuring his claws. Ariel endured this regimen in pained silence. She even took him for rides in her car. But Ariel simply sat silently in the seat beside her.

She was always trying to get
him to talk, but Ariel refused to
say a word.

Her friends came by to admire
him.

"Can he talk?" they asked.

"Oh, yes," Lou Ella answered,
"of course he can. But he's a bit
shy in front of company."

Privately she went on urging
him to speak, but she was not a
patient lady.

"Come on, why don't you say
something? The man at the pet
shop assured me that you were a
very good talker. So why don't you

say 'Pretty Polly' or 'Who's a clever boy, then?' as other parrots do?"

But Ariel remained stubbornly silent, hunched on his perch.

One morning, when Percy was helping Digby to shore up a bit of collapsing trellis near Lou Ella's garden wall, they saw Ariel pacing restlessly up and down.

"Good morning!" Digby called out.

And, to his surprise, Ariel answered back: "Good morning to you, sir!"

"I didn't know you could speak!" said Digby, in astonishment.

"Of course I can," Ariel replied. "But I just don't care for Lou Ella's boring conversation. She keeps trying to make me say silly, pointless things. She doesn't seem to realize that I am a highly educated bird. It's humiliating! My confidence is getting so low, I've almost forgotten how to fly."

After this meeting, Digby, Percy, and Ariel often chatted together over the garden wall when Lou Ella was out. And Digby and Percy soon discovered that Ariel was indeed a very interesting bird, with many hidden talents.

There's excitement in store
for Digby, Percy, and Ariel.
The intrepid threesome become
friends and go off on a special
day out to the big air show. And
before long, they are swept away on
an adventure in the clouds. . . .

Find out what happens next in
DiGBY O'DAY
Up, Up, and Away!

TO EVERY THING
THERE IS A SEASON

OTHER BOOKS BY ALISTAIR MacLEOD

The Lost Salt Gift of Blood
As Birds Bring Forth the Sun
No Great Mischief: A Novel
Island: The Collected Stories

TO EVERY THING
THERE IS A SEASON

A CAPE BRETON CHRISTMAS STORY

ALISTAIR MacLEOD

WITH ILLUSTRATIONS BY PETER RANKIN

A DOUGLAS GIBSON BOOK

M&S

National Library of Canada Cataloguing in Publication

MacLeod, Alistair
To every thing there is a season : a Cape Breton Christmas story / Alistair MacLeod ; Peter Rankin, illustrator.

"A Douglas Gibson book"

ISBN 0-7710-5565-X

1. Christmas stories, Canadian (English)   2. Cape Breton Island (N.S.) – Fiction.   I. Rankin, Peter, 1961-   II. Title.

PS8575.L459T6 2004   C813´.54   C2004-901116-2

We acknowledge the financial support of the Government of Canada through the Book Publishing Industry Development Program and that of the government of Ontario through the Ontario Media Development Corporation's Ontario Book Initiative. We further acknowledge the support of the Canada Council for the Arts and the Ontario Arts Council for our publishing program.

Typeset in Bembo by M&S, Toronto
Printed and bound in Canada

This book is printed on acid-free paper that is
100% ancient forest-friendly (100% post-consumer recycled)

A Douglas Gibson Book
McClelland & Stewart Ltd.
The Canadian Publishers
481 University Avenue
Toronto, Ontario
M5G 2E9
www.mcclelland.com

1 2 3 4 5   08 07 06 05 04

TO EVERY THING
THERE IS A SEASON

TO EVERY THING THERE IS A SEASON

A History

Since it is likely that this little book will make its way to the ends of the earth, there will be readers who would like to know more about the corner of the world in which it is set. Cape Breton Island forms the northern part of Nova Scotia, a province on Canada's Atlantic shore. Ever since Cape Breton was joined to the mainland by the Canso causeway in 1955, it has not been physically an island, but to its people it has remained an island of the mind.

These people came from many parts of the world. Some are descended from the native people who have lived here for thousands of years. Others are Acadians, descendants of those who clung on

here after all the French-speaking settlers had sup-
posedly been expelled in the ebb and flow of the
French-English wars. Another war, the American
Revolution, brought the refugees known as Loyal-
ists from south of the new border in search of a
new home. And many countries in Europe are rep-
resented by the others who were later attracted by
work in the coal mines or steel mills of the area.

But the largest group is descended from the
Highland Scots who came here fleeing harsh conditions in the eighteenth and nineteenth centuries.
Hugh MacLennan, another great writer from Cape
Breton, has written in anger about the reasons for
their arrival: "When the English set out to destroy
the clans of Scotland, the most independent of the
Highlanders left their homes with the pipes playing
laments on the decks of their ships. They crossed the
ocean and the pipes played again when they waded
ashore on the rocky coast of Cape Breton Island."

MacLennan went on to write in the Introduction

to *Each Man's Son* about the beauty of the Island: "Inland were high hills and a loch running in from the sea that looked like a sleeve of gold in the afternoon sun. There were trout and salmon streams lined by sweet-smelling alder, water meadows and valleys graced by elms as stately as those in the shires of southern England. The coast was rugged with gray granite or red sandstone cliffs, splendid with promontories, fog-bound in the spring when the drift ice came down from Newfoundland and Labrador, tranquil in summer, and in the autumns thunderous with evidences of the power of the Lord."

These were Alistair MacLeod's people down through many generations and they are the people about whom he writes. Most of the families, if they did not live in the town or work in the mines, would have a small farm where cows and sheep and pigs and hens and a small garden provided a living. Things would be easier with the help of the wages of a husband or son who worked on the fishing boats or in the woods or, like young Neil in the story, on "the lake boats" in Ontario. But however hard the life was, however many sons and daughters were forced to leave in search of work, the people belonged to the land, loved it, and returned to it down through the generations. And their music still stretches across the world tying together those who hear it, taking them back to Cape Breton.

To an outsider it sometimes seems that everyone in Cape Breton is related to everyone else. It is notable that Peter Rankin, the illustrator of this book, is part of the clan that, as The Rankin Family, has helped to spread Cape Breton's music. By happy chance Peter's specialty is researching and illustrating the way of life in rural Cape Breton a generation or two ago. Although he is still a young man, born in 1961, he remembers growing up in a house with no television, where the radio was the centre of news and information, and

the entertainment sprang from the people gathered around the stove or the kitchen table. He knows well the scenes that he shows here.

As for Alistair MacLeod, he has made it clear that this story refers back, not to his own family directly, but to the times when he was growing up in the 1940s on the west coast of Cape Breton. In those days, many things were still done in the old way, and horses were still used to draw sleighs, sharing the road with cars. In many respects the life he writes about here is almost unchanged from the life of a Cape Breton family in earlier decades, even in an earlier century. This little family waiting for Christmas exists in a timeless world.

The story first appeared in the *Globe and Mail* in Toronto on December 24, 1977. It was first published in book form in 1986 when it was included in the collection *As Birds Bring Forth the Sun*. Later, after the publication of *No Great Mischief* had brought Alistair MacLeod's work to the attention of a worldwide audience, this story was included in the 2000 collection of all of his stories, *Island*.

From the moment of its first appearance "To Every Thing There Is a Season" has been hailed as a classic story, one that will last for all time.

 *I am speaking here of a time when I was eleven and lived with my family on our small farm on the west coast of Cape Breton. My family had been there for a long, long time and so it seemed had I. And much of that time seems like the proverbial yesterday. Yet when I speak on this Christmas 1977, I am not sure how much I speak with the voice of that time or how much in the voice of what I have since become. And I am not sure how many liberties I may be taking with the boy I think I was. For Christmas is a time of both past and present and often the two are imperfectly blended. As we step into its nowness we often look behind.*

We have been waiting now, it seems, forever. Actually, it has been most intense since Hallowe'en when the first snow fell upon us as we moved like muffled mummers upon darkened country roads. The large flakes were soft and new then and almost generous, and the earth to which they fell was still warm and as yet unfrozen. They fell in silence into the puddles and into the sea where they disappeared at the moment of contact. They disappeared, too, upon touching the heated redness of our necks and hands or the faces of those who did not wear masks. We carried our pillowcases from house to house, knocking on doors to become silhouettes in the light thrown out from kitchens (white pillowcases held out by whitened forms). The snow fell between us and the doors and was transformed in shimmering golden beams. When we turned to leave, it fell upon our footprints, and as the night wore on

obliterated them and all the records of our move-
ments. In the morning everything was soft and still
and November had come upon us.

My brother Kenneth, who is two and a half, is
unsure of his last Christmas. It is Hallowe'en that
looms largest in his memory as an exceptional time
of being up late in magic darkness and falling snow.
"Who are you going to dress up as at Christmas?"
he asks. "I think I'll be a snowman." All of us laugh
at that and tell him Santa Claus will find him if he
is good and that he need not dress up at all. We go
about our appointed tasks waiting for it to happen.

I am troubled myself about the nature of Santa
Claus and I am trying to hang on to him in any
way that I can. It is true that at my age I no longer
really believe in him, yet I have hoped in all his
possibilities as fiercely as I can; much in the same
way, I think, that the drowning man waves desperately to the lights of the passing ship on the high
sea's darkness. For without him, as without the

man's ship, it seems our fragile lives would be so much more desperate.

My mother has been fairly tolerant of my attempted perpetuation. Perhaps because she has encountered it before. Once I overheard her speaking about my sister Anne to one of her neighbours. "I thought Anne would believe forever," she said. "I practically had to tell her." I have somehow always wished I had not heard her say that as I seek sanctuary and reinforcement even in an ignorance I know I dare not trust.

Kenneth, however, believes with an unadulterated fervour, and so do Bruce and Barry, who are six-year-old twins. Beyond me there is Anne who is thirteen and Mary who is fifteen, both of whom seem to be leaving childhood at an alarming rate. My mother has told us that she was already married when she was seventeen, which is only two years older than Mary is now. That, too, seems strange to contemplate and perhaps childhood is shorter for

some than it is for others. I think of this sometimes in the evenings when we have finished our chores and the supper dishes have been cleared away and we are supposed to be doing our homework. I glance sideways at my mother, who is always knitting or mending, and at my father, who mostly sits by the stove coughing quietly with his handkerchief at his mouth. He has "not been well" for over two years and has difficulty breathing whenever he moves at more than the slowest pace. He is most sympathetic of all concerning my extended hopes, and says we should hang on to the good things in our lives as long as we are able. As I look at him out of the corner of my eye, it does not seem that he has many of them left. He is old, we think, at forty-two.

Yet Christmas, in spite of all the doubts of our different ages, is a fine and splendid time, and now as we pass the midpoint of December our expectations are heightened by the increasing coldness that has settled down upon us. The ocean is flat and calm

and along the coast, in the scooped-out coves, has turned to an icy slush. The brook that flows past our house is almost totally frozen and there is only a small channel of rushing water that flows openly at its very centre. When we let the cattle out to drink, we chop holes with the axe at the brook's edge so that they can drink without venturing onto the ice.

The sheep move in and out of their lean-to shelter, restlessly stamping their feet or huddling together in tightly packed groups. A conspiracy of wool against the cold. The hens perch high on their roosts with their feathers fluffed out about them, hardly feeling it worthwhile to descend to the floor for their few scant kernels of grain. The pig, who has little time before his butchering, squeals his displeasure to the cold and with his snout tosses his wooden trough high in the icy air. The splendid young horse paws the planking of his stall and gnaws the wooden cribwork of his manger.

We have put a protective barricade of spruce
boughs about our kitchen door and banked our
house with additional boughs and billows of eel
grass. Still, the pail of water we leave standing
in the porch is solid in the morning and has to

be broken with the hammer.
The clothes my mother hangs
on the line are frozen almost
instantly and sway and creak
from their suspending clothes-
pins like sections of dismantled
robots: the stiff-legged rasping trousers and the
shirts and sweaters with unyielding arms out-
stretched. In the morning we race from our frigid
upstairs bedrooms to finish dressing around the
kitchen stove.

We would extend our coldness half a continent
away to the Great Lakes of Ontario so that it might
hasten the Christmas coming of my oldest brother,
Neil. He is nineteen and employed on the "lake

boats," the long flat carriers of grain and iron ore whose season ends any day after December 10, depending on the ice conditions. We wish it to be cold, cold on the Great Lakes of Ontario, so that he may come home to us as soon as possible. Already his cartons have arrived. They come from different places: Cobourg, Toronto, St. Catharines, Welland, Windsor, Sarnia, Sault Ste. Marie. Places that we, with the exception of my father, have never been. We locate them excitedly on the map, tracing their outlines with eager fingers. The cartons bear the lettering of Canada Steamship Lines, and are bound with rope knotted intricately in the fashion of sailors. My mother says they contain his "clothes" and we are not allowed to open them.

For us it is impossible to know the time or manner of his coming. If the lakes freeze early, he may come by train because it is cheaper. If the lakes stay open until December 20, he will have to fly because his time will be more precious than his money. He will hitchhike the last sixty or hundred miles from either station or airport. On our part, we can do nothing but listen with straining ears to radio reports of distant ice formations. His coming seems to depend on so many factors which are out there far beyond us and over which we lack control.

The days go by in fevered slowness until finally on the morning of December 23 the strange car rolls into our yard. My mother touches her hand to her lips and whispers "Thank God." My father gets up unsteadily from his chair to look through the window. Their longed-for son and our golden older brother is here at last. He is here with his reddish hair and beard and we can hear his hearty laugh. He will be happy and strong and confident for us all.

There are three other young men with him who look much the same as he. They, too, are from the boats and are trying to get home to Newfoundland. They must still drive a hundred miles to reach the ferry at North Sydney. The car seems very old. They purchased it in Thorold for two hundred dollars because they were too late to make any reservations, and they have driven steadily since they began. In northern New Brunswick their windshield wipers failed, but instead of stopping they tied lengths of cord to the wipers' arms and passed them through the front window vents. Since that time, in whatever precipitation, one of them has pulled the cords back and forth to make the wipers function. This information falls tiredly but excitedly from their lips and we greedily gather it in. My father pours them drinks of rum and

my mother takes out her mincemeat and the fruit-cakes she has been carefully hoarding. We lean on the furniture or look from the safety of sheltered doorways. We would like to hug our brother but are too shy with strangers present. In the kitchen's warmth, the young men begin to nod and doze, their heads dropping suddenly to their chests. They nudge each other with their feet in an attempt to keep awake. They will not stay and rest because they have come so far and tomorrow is Christmas Eve and stretches of mountains and water still lie

between them and those they love. After they leave we pounce upon our brother physically and verbally. He laughs and shouts and lifts us over his head and swings us in his muscular arms. Yet in spite of his happiness he seems surprised at the appearance of his father, whom he has not

seen since March. My father merely smiles at him, while my mother bites her lip.

Now that he is here there is a great flurry of activity. We have left everything we could until the time he might be with us. Eagerly I show him the fir tree on the hill which I have been watching for months and marvel at how easily he fells it and carries it down the hill. We fall over one another in the excitement of decoration.

He promises that on Christmas Eve he will take us to church in the sleigh behind the splendid horse that until his coming we are all afraid to handle. And on the afternoon of Christmas Eve he shoes the horse, lifting each hoof and rasping it fine and hammering the cherry-red horseshoes into shape upon the anvil. Later he drops them hissingly into the steaming tub of water. My father sits beside him on an overturned pail and tells him what to do. Sometimes we argue with our father, but our brother does everything he says.

That night, bundled in hay and voluminous coats, and with heated stones at our feet, we start upon our journey. Our parents and Kenneth remain at home, but all the rest of us go. Before we leave we feed the cattle and sheep and even the pig all that they can possibly eat, so that they will be contented on Christmas Eve. Our parents wave to us from the doorway. We go four miles across the mountain road. It is a primitive logging trail and there will be no cars or other vehicles upon it. At first the horse is wild with excitement and lack of exercise and my brother has to stand at the front of the sleigh and lean backwards on the reins. Later he settles down to a trot and still later to a walk as the mountain rises before him. We sing all the Christmas songs we know and watch for the rabbits and foxes scudding across the open patches of snow

and listen to the drumming of partridge wings. We are never cold.

When we descend to the country church we tie the horse in a grove of trees where he will be sheltered and not frightened by the many cars. We put a blanket over him and give him oats. At the church door the neighbours shake hands with my brother. "Hello, Neil," they say. "How is your father?"

"Oh," he says, just "Oh."

The church is very beautiful at night with its festooned branches and glowing candles and the booming, joyous sounds that come from the choir loft. We go through the service as if we are mesmerized.

On the way home, although the stones have cooled, we remain happy and warm. We listen to the creak of the leather harness and the hiss of runners on the snow and begin to think of the potentiality of presents. When we are about a mile from home the horse senses his destination and breaks into a trot and then into a confident lope. My brother lets him go and we move across the winter landscape like figures freed from a Christmas card. The snow from the horse's hooves falls about our heads like the whiteness of the stars.

After we have stabled the horse we talk with our parents and eat the meal our mother has prepared. And then I am sleepy and it is time for the younger children to be in bed. But tonight my father says to me, "We would like you to stay up with us a while," and so I stay quietly with the older members of my family.

When all is silent upstairs Neil brings in the cartons that contain his "clothes" and begins to open them. He unties the intricate knots quickly, their whorls falling away before his agile fingers. The boxes are filled with gifts neatly wrapped and bearing tags. The ones for my younger brothers say "from Santa Claus" but mine are not among them any more, as I know with certainty they will never

be again. Yet I am not so much surprised as touched by a pang of loss at being here on the adult side of the world. It is as if I have suddenly moved into another room and heard a door click lastingly behind me. I am jabbed by my own small wound.

But then I look at those before me. I look at my parents drawn together before the Christmas tree. My mother has her hand upon my father's shoulder and he is holding his ever-present handkerchief. I look at my sisters, who have crossed this threshold ahead of me and now each day journey farther from the lives they knew as girls. I look at my magic older brother who has come to us this Christmas from half a continent away, bringing everything he has and is. All of them are captured in the tableau of their care.

"Every man moves on," says my father quietly, and I think he speaks of Santa Claus, "but there is no need to grieve. He leaves good things behind."

ABOUT THE AUTHOR

Alistair MacLeod

Alistair MacLeod was born in North Battleford, Saskatchewan, in 1936 and was raised among an extended family in Cape Breton, Nova Scotia. He still spends his summers in Inverness County, writing in a clifftop cabin looking west towards Prince Edward Island. In his early years, to finance his education he worked as a logger, a miner, and a fisherman, and writes vividly and sympathetically about such work.

Until his retirement in 2000, Dr. MacLeod spent all of the winter months as a professor of English at the University of Windsor, Ontario. His early studies were at the Nova Scotia Teachers College,

St. Francis Xavier University, the University of New Brunswick, and Notre Dame, where he took his Ph.D. He has also taught creative writing at the University of Indiana. Working alongside W.O. Mitchell, he was an inspiring teacher to generations of writers at the Banff Centre.

He was sixty-four years old when in 1999 he published his first novel, *No Great Mischief*, with its ringing final line "All of us are better when we're loved." Until the novel appeared his published fiction consisted of only two books containing fourteen short stories in all, including "To Every Thing There Is a Season."

Among many other prizes, *No Great Mischief* won the IMPAC Award in Dublin, the world's richest literary prize. The book appeared in translation in many countries around the world and the attendant fame happily contradicted Michael Ondaatje's earlier description of him as "one of the great undiscovered writers of our time." His short story collection,

Island, containing all of his short stories, appeared in 2000 and also became a major best-seller.

Alistair MacLeod has given lectures and readings from his work in many cities in Canada and around the world. He and his wife, Anita, have six children and two grandchildren. They live in Windsor.

ABOUT THE ILLUSTRATOR

Peter Rankin

Peter Rankin was born in Cape Breton, Nova Scotia, in 1961 and grew up in Mabou Harbour and Mabou Coal Mines in a family of fourteen children. It was a traditional upbringing. "Gaelic was spoken often in our home and was my father's first language," he recalls. "Gaelic songs, fiddle music and storytelling were some of the many pastimes we enjoyed as children."

His grandmother was an accomplished artist, a creator of prized hooked rugs, and young Peter's drawings and paintings were so promising that some of his work was published when he was in high school. He then took a B.A. at St. Francis

Xavier University and moved to Halifax, where he became a professional artist.

In time he returned to Cape Breton to become a fisherman, but he combines that work with his life as an artist. Traditional Cape Breton rural life is his favourite subject, and he has written, "I enjoy taking part in the work of a rural lifestyle, from working in the boats, the woods, the farm, carpentry or whatever. I feel that my artwork can then have that authenticity that comes from knowing and doing."

Making Room, a book for children by Joanne Taylor with Peter Rankin's illustrations, was published by Tundra Books in 2004.

He lives in Mabou Coal Mines with his wife and their five children.

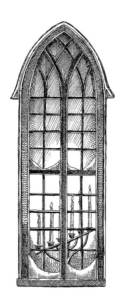